KRAKATOA

Sue Graves

RISING STARS

Rising Stars UK Ltd.
22 Grafton Street, London W1S 4EX
www.risingstars-uk.com

nasen

NASEN House, 4/5 Amber Business Village, Amber Close,
Amington, Tamworth, Staffordshire B77 4RP

Published 2009

Cover design: pentacor**big**
Illustrations: Rob Lenihan, So Creative Ltd and Paul Loudon
Text design and typesetting: pentacor**big**
Publisher: Gill Budgell
Editorial project management: Lucy Poddington
Editorial consultant: Lorraine Petersen

British Library Cataloguing in Publication Data.
A CIP record for this book is available from the British Library.

ISBN: 978-1-84680-490-8

Printed by Craft Print International Limited, Singapore

CHAPTER 1

Chris Wilson, the boss at Dangerous Games, was away on holiday for four weeks. Janet Winter, his assistant, was in charge while he was away. She was in a terrible mood. Kojo had been late for work three days in a row. Janet wanted to see him in her office right away.

JANET WINTER

Kojo was really worried.

"I hope she doesn't sack me," he said to Tom and Sima.

Sima and Tom worked with Kojo. They made computer games together and they were good mates.

"It'll be OK," said Sima. She gave Kojo a hug. "Just tell her you're sorry and that you won't be late again."

Kojo went into Janet Winter's office. Sima and Tom heard her shouting at him.

"Uh-oh!" said Sima. "Things don't sound too good."

The door opened and Kojo came out.

"What happened?" asked Tom. "Did she sack you?"

"No," said Kojo. "But she really lost it. She was like a volcano erupting. I couldn't wait to get out of there. I'm never going to be late for work again after that!"

Sima sat down at her desk. She was thinking hard. Then she started to do some drawings.

"What are you up to?" asked Tom.

"Kojo's given me an idea for a new game," she said.

Tom grinned. "You mean a computer game where you have to escape from an angry boss?"

"No, not quite," laughed Sima. "It's a game where you have to escape from an erupting volcano."

"That would be awesome!" said Tom. "Why don't we test the game for real, like we've done before?"

"Hmm!" said Sima. "I'm not sure about that. Let me see how these designs work out. I'll let you know later on."

CHAPTER 2

Later that day, Sima showed her designs to Kojo and Tom.

"The game begins on a volcano," Sima explained. "You have to find a way off the volcano before it erupts. It'll be brilliant, but scary! I've planned a safe version which we can test for real. We won't be in any danger."

"Nice one, Sima," said Tom.

"I'll program it right away," said Kojo.

He took the designs to his computer and set to work. Then he had an idea. "Why don't we set the game in the past?" he said.

"What difference would that make?" asked Tom.

"Probably not much," said Kojo. "But we've never tried it before and it might be more exciting. What do you think, Sima?"

"Go for it," said Sima. "Choose a year and we'll see what happens."

A few days later, Kojo had finished programming the game. That evening, when everyone else had gone home, Tom, Sima and Kojo got ready to test it.

"Do we get any special outfits in this game?" asked Tom.

"Sorry, not this time," Sima replied.

"Boring!" sighed Tom.

"You'll love the game," said Sima. "I promise."

Kojo checked his watch. "OK, guys," he said. "You know the score. We all have to touch the screen at the same time. And remember, the game only finishes when we hear the words 'Game over'."

Sima and Tom nodded.

They all touched the screen together. A bright light flashed, hurting their eyes. They shut them tightly.

CHAPTER 3

When Tom, Kojo and Sima opened their eyes, they were standing on the side of a huge mountain. They looked around. The mountain was on an island in the middle of the sea. There were two other mountains on the island as well. But they weren't ordinary mountains – they were all volcanoes. Steam was shooting out of cracks in the ground.

59:00
WHAT A WEIRD PLACE. THE ISLAND IS MADE UP OF THREE VOLCANOES AND NOTHING ELSE. IT LOOKS REALLY DANGEROUS.
WHY ARE YOU SURPRISED? YOU DESIGNED THE GAME. YOU MUST HAVE DRAWN IT LIKE THIS.
NO, I DIDN'T DESIGN THIS STRANGE ISLAND. I JUST DREW A MASSIVE VOLCANO.

Tom scratched his head and thought for a moment. "These three volcanoes remind me of a project I did at school, years ago," he said.

"What was it about?" asked Sima.

"A volcano called Krakatoa. It was an island just like this," said Tom. "Let me see …" He got out his mobile phone and did a quick web search. "Yeah, here we go – it exploded in 1883."

Kojo gulped. "What did you say?" he spluttered.

"I said Krakatoa exploded in 1883," said Tom. "Why, what's up?"

Kojo looked worried. "That was the year I programmed into the game," he said. "I typed in a time and a date. It was 12pm, 26–08–1883."

Tom's mouth dropped open. "You did what?" he said. "If this is Krakatoa, we're in a very dangerous place. In August 1883 the whole island blew apart. It was one of the biggest explosions ever recorded. I've got a nasty feeling we're standing on it on the very day it explodes!"

53:00
I'M AN IDIOT. I THOUGHT THAT DATE SOUNDED FAMILIAR SOMEHOW!

A loud rumbling noise came from deep inside the volcano.

Sima began to climb down the side of the mountain. Tom and Kojo followed close behind.

"I don't suppose you can find out what time the volcano erupted, can you?" asked Sima.

"Hang on," said Tom. He checked the website again. "It says here that a long series of explosions started at about 1pm on 26th August. A day later most of the island was gone. It had been completely blown apart."

A huge bang made them all jump. The earth shook under their feet.

Kojo looked at his watch.

45:00
WE'VE ONLY GOT 45 MINUTES TO GET OFF THIS MOUNTAIN BEFORE WE'RE ALL KILLED!

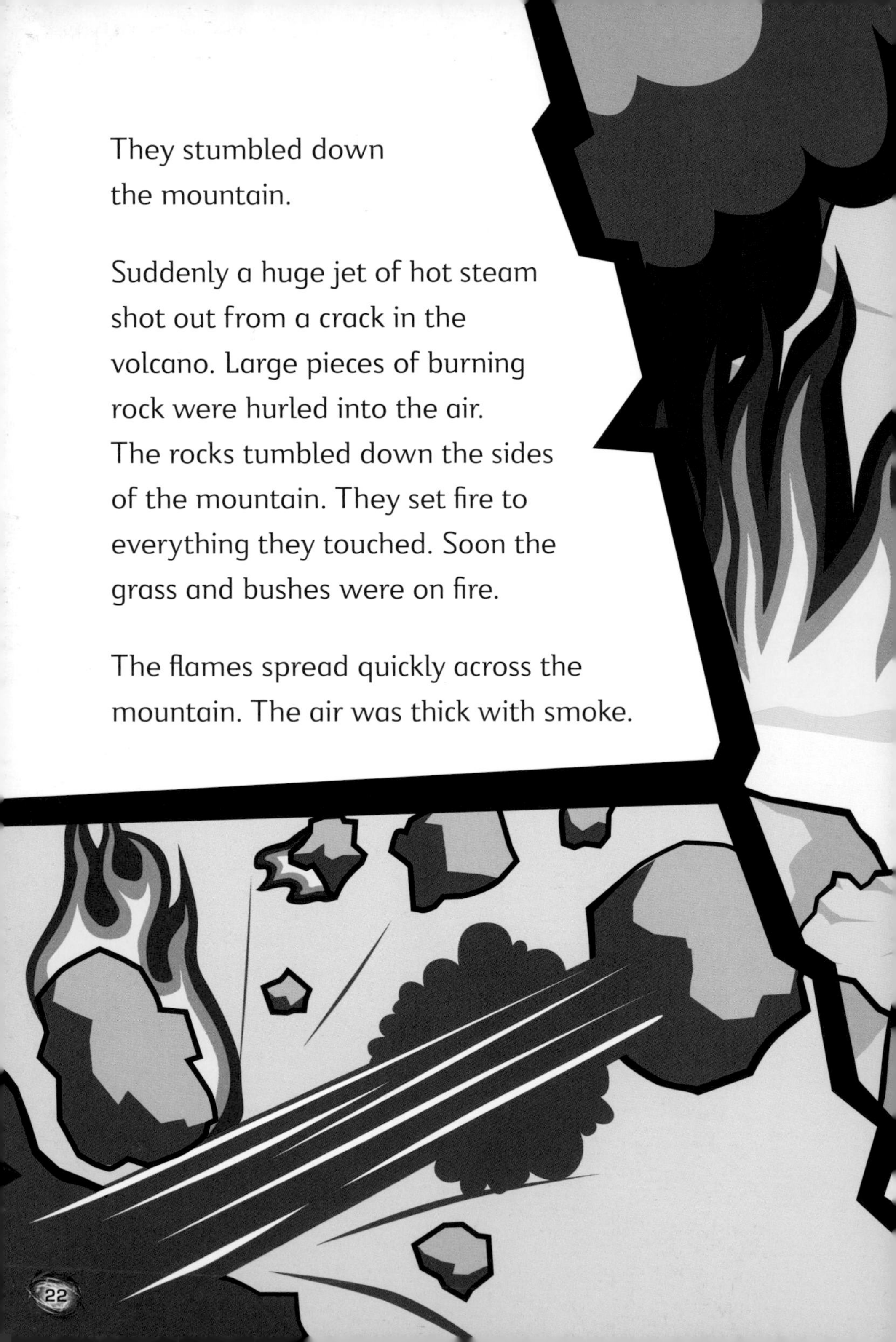

They stumbled down
the mountain.

Suddenly a huge jet of hot steam
shot out from a crack in the
volcano. Large pieces of burning
rock were hurled into the air.
The rocks tumbled down the sides
of the mountain. They set fire to
everything they touched. Soon the
grass and bushes were on fire.

The flames spread quickly across the
mountain. The air was thick with smoke.

31:00

The smoke made it hard to breathe.
Sima began to choke.

Tom rushed over to help her. He pulled off his T-shirt and pushed it into her hands.

Sima held the T-shirt up to her face.

Kojo looked down the mountainside. The flames were spreading out. There was no way down. They were trapped!

27:00
COVER YOUR MOUTH AND NOSE WITH THIS. IT'LL HELP TO KEEP THE SMOKE OUT.

Sima pointed to a deep gully running down the side of the mountain. The flames hadn't got into the gully yet.

They ran towards it. But Kojo tripped and fell over. His jacket caught fire. Tom ran over to him. He pulled the jacket off Kojo and threw it as far away as he could. They watched as the jacket burnt up in a split second.

"That was close!" said Kojo.

Tom pulled him to his feet. "Come on," he said. "Run for the gully."

22:00

CHAPTER 4

Sima, Tom and Kojo climbed into the gully. They watched as the flames closed in over them.

Sima looked down the gully. It was a long way to the bottom of the mountain.

"We must try and get to that rocky ledge by the sea," she said. "Once we're off the mountain, the game will end and we'll be safe."

"We've got to get there before the volcano turns us into toast!" said Tom. "We've seen nothing yet. In 15 minutes the explosions are really going to kick off."

15:00

Carefully, Tom, Sima and Kojo climbed down the gully. The sides of it were hot to touch. Small jets of steam shot out from cracks in the rock.

Sima began to feel very scared. "We've got to go faster," she said. "We're not going to make it if we don't speed up."

She tried to climb down faster, but her foot slipped. She slid into a deep crack. Just then a boulder tipped forward, trapping her behind it.

Tom and Kojo climbed down to help her. They tried to push the boulder away, but it wouldn't move.

09:00
I CAN'T GET OUT.
I CAN'T MOVE!
DON'T PANIC!
WE'LL GET YOU
OUT.

Kojo pushed again at the boulder, but nothing happened.

Then Tom spotted a flat piece of rock. It gave him an idea. He pushed it under the boulder.

"On the count of three, we both jump on the flat rock," said Tom. "It should work as a lever to lift up the boulder. Then Sima can squeeze out from behind it. Are you ready?"

"Ready!" said Kojo.

Tom gave the signal. They both jumped on the flat piece of rock and the boulder lifted up. There was just enough space for Sima to squeeze past.

07:00
ONE, TWO, THREE!

Kojo looked at his watch. The minutes were ticking by. Now there were only five minutes left. But they still had a long way to go before they could get off the mountain.

He shook his head sadly and sat down on a rock.

05:00

Tom climbed a little way up the side of the gully. The flames on one side had burnt out. The ground was very hot but it was not on fire.

"I've got an idea," he said. "We're going to roll down the mountain."

"Are you crazy?" said Kojo. "Or do you want to die?"

Sima pulled Kojo to his feet.

They climbed out of the gully and lay down on the hot ash. They could feel the heat through their clothes.

"Tuck in your head and knees," said Tom. "Hold on tightly to each other. Are you ready?"

"As ready as I'll ever be!" said Kojo grimly.

CHAPTER 5

The three of them rolled down the mountain. They sent up clouds of hot ash as they rolled down. The ash filled their mouths and noses. It stung their eyes. But they didn't let go of each other.

02:00

WE MADE IT!
TOM, YOU'RE A GENIUS!

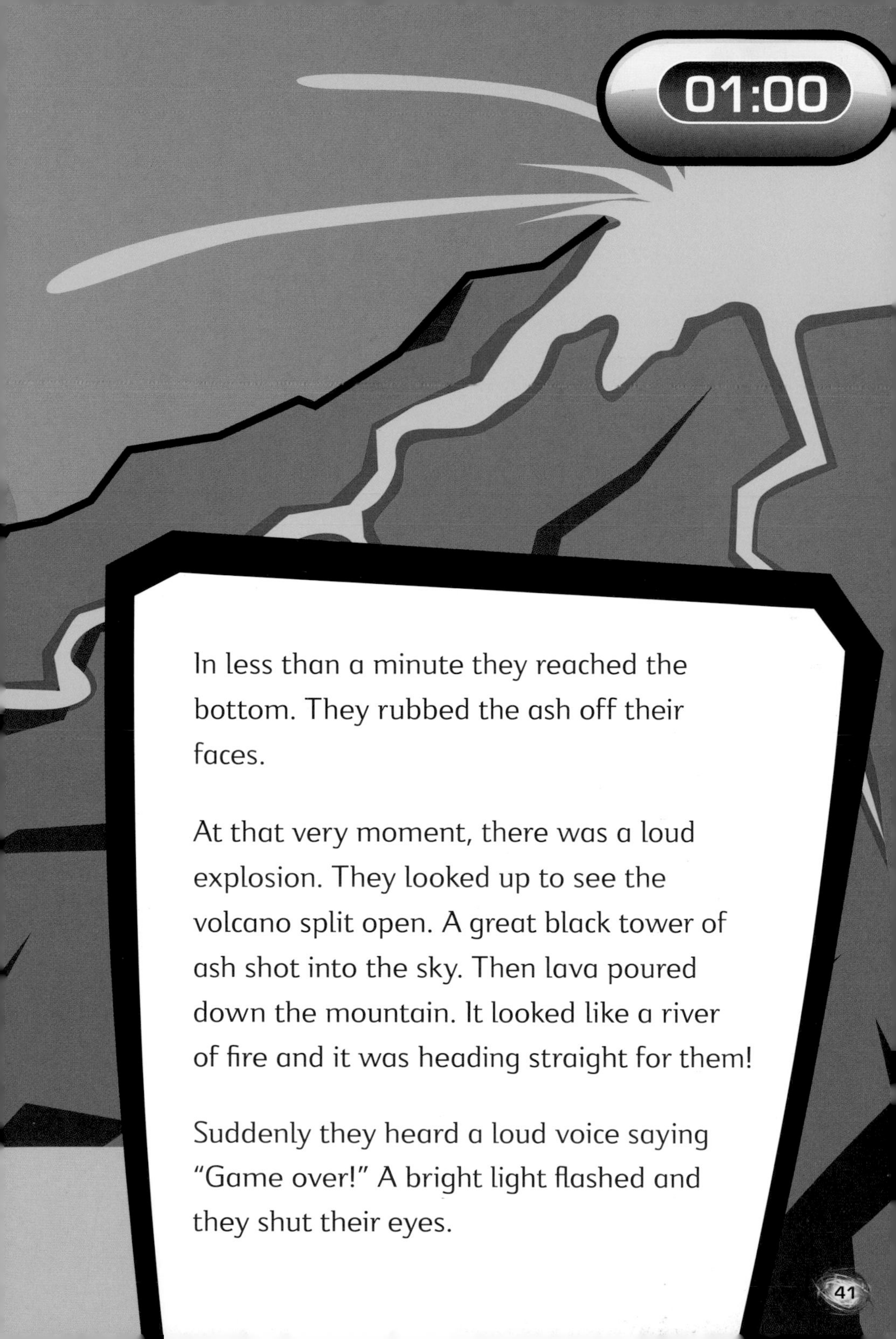

In less than a minute they reached the bottom. They rubbed the ash off their faces.

At that very moment, there was a loud explosion. They looked up to see the volcano split open. A great black tower of ash shot into the sky. Then lava poured down the mountain. It looked like a river of fire and it was heading straight for them!

Suddenly they heard a loud voice saying "Game over!" A bright light flashed and they shut their eyes.

They found themselves back in the office.
They were safe.

"That explosion was amazing!" said Tom as he brushed ash from his hair.

"I can't believe we survived Krakatoa. What a buzz!" added Kojo.

"Yeah, but there's just one thing, Kojo," said Sima.

"What's that?" he asked.

"Please reprogram the game and take out the date. It wasn't one of your best ideas!"

Just then Janet Winter came in. She sniffed the air. She looked furious.

"I can smell smoke!" said Janet. "You know that it's against the law to smoke anywhere in this building."

"But we don't smoke!" said Sima.

"Then where has all this ash come from?" Janet snapped.

"We got too near a volcano," said Tom and he winked at Sima.

Janet glared at him. "Very funny! I'll see you in my office tomorrow morning, Thomas. Now clear up this mess." She walked off.

"Looks like you're in for another erupting volcano tomorrow, Tom," said Sima.

"Sooner you than me!" said Kojo, laughing.

Glossary of terms

ash a powder that is left when something has burnt

erupt to explode

gully a long, narrow crack in a mountainside

jet a stream of liquid or gas that comes out of something with a lot of force

lava hot, liquid rock that comes out of a volcano

lever a handle you press to make something move

program to write a computer game or other computer program

steam a white mist made up of tiny droplets of water

volcano a mountain that sends out lava and ash from inside the earth

Quiz

1 Why wasn't Chris Wilson in the office?

2 What was the name of his assistant?

3 Why did Kojo have to go and see her?

4 What was the name of the volcano in the game?

5 How many volcanoes formed the island?

6 Whose idea was it to get into the gully?

7 Whose jacket caught fire?

8 What trapped Sima in the gully?

9 How did they get down the volcano in the end?

10 What did Janet think Tom, Sima and Kojo had been doing in the office?

About the Author

Sue Graves has taught for thirty years in Cheshire schools. She has been writing for more than ten years and has written well over a hundred books for children and young adults.

"Nearly everyone loves computer games. They are popular with all age groups – especially young adults. But I've often thought it would be amazing to play a computer game for real. To be in on the action would be the best experience ever! That's why I wrote these stories. I hope you enjoy reading them as much as I've enjoyed writing them for you."

Answers to Quiz

1 He was on holiday for four weeks

2 Janet Winter

3 He'd been late for work three days in a row

4 Krakatoa

5 Three

6 Sima's

7 Kojo's

8 A boulder

9 They rolled down

10 She thought they'd been smoking